WILLIAM SHAKESPEARE'S
HAMLET

Retold by BRUCE COVILLE

Pictures by LEONID GORE

Dial Books | *New York*

Published by Dial Books
A member of Penguin Group (USA) Inc.
345 Hudson Street • New York, New York 10014

Text copyright © 2004 by Bruce Coville
Pictures copyright © 2004 by Leonid Gore
All rights reserved
Designed by Atha Tehon
Text set in Bembo
Manufactured in China on acid-free paper
1 3 5 7 9 10 8 6 4 2

Library of Congress Cataloging-in-Publication Data
Coville, Bruce.
William Shakespeare's Hamlet / retold by Bruce Coville;
pictures by Leonid Gore.
p.   cm.
Summary: Retells, in simplified prose, William Shakespeare's play
about a prince of Denmark who seeks revenge for his father's murder.
ISBN 0-8037-2708-9
1. Hamlet (Legendary character)—Juvenile fiction.
2. Revenge—Juvenile fiction. 3. Denmark—Juvenile fiction.
4. Princes—Juvenile fiction.
[1. Shakespeare, William, 1564–1616—Adaptations.]
I. Shakespeare, William, 1564–1616. Hamlet.
II. Gore, Leonid, ill. III. Title.
PR2878.H3 C68 2004   822.3'3—dc21   2002013743

The paintings were done in acrylic and pastel on paper.

For Daniel Bostick — Great Actor, Great Friend
B.C.

To Atha Tehon, for sharing the doubts
L.G.

OF ALL Shakespeare's works, *Hamlet* is arguably the greatest. Certainly it is the most well known, and probably the most frequently quoted. And what quotations! Line after singing line has entered the common parlance, including what is probably the single most famous line ever penned in the English language: "To be, or not to be, that is the question."

But it's not just the glory of its language that has kept *Hamlet* alive for over four hundred years. The play itself is endlessly fascinating, so much so that a reader or viewer or performer can come back to it a hundred times without ever plumbing all of its depths. (Indeed, I have been flinging myself against its mysteries for over thirty years now, and it still reveals new meanings each time I read or see it.)

Yet all too often when *Hamlet* is taught, we spend so much time working our way through that richness of language—exploring the mysteries of its metaphors, so to speak—that we lose sight of what a compelling story we have before us, a breakneck tale of ghosts, murder, madness, and revenge. One of my goals in this adaptation has been to give young readers a chance to experience *Hamlet* as story before they begin the deeper explorations that can add so much richness to repeated experiences of the play.

It is ironic that in our justifiable admiration for Shakespeare's genius we have done him a disservice by making his writing seem inaccessible, or something to be worked at rather than enjoyed. He was, after all, a man of the theater, and always strove to entertain—as do we with this volume, which, like all the others in this line, is meant to provide an enjoyable hint of the greater wonders still in store when *Hamlet* is seen in performance, or read in its entirety.

LATE one fog-shrouded night three men stood watch on the battlements of Elsinore castle. The castle was on high alert, for rumors were spreading that Fortinbras of Norway was preparing to attack Denmark.

Yet this night the men watched for something more than an approaching army.

They watched for a ghost.

In the darkest hours the phantom appeared, a spectral shade whose chill, silent presence struck fear into their hearts.

"Hamlet must be told of this!" whispered Horatio, who had been brought by the other two men to observe the specter.

Hamlet was Horatio's closest friend. He was also the prince of Denmark, and the ghost the men had seen was that of his father, who had died less than two months before.

The prince had not taken the throne upon his father's death because at that time Denmark's kings were elected by the nobles. Hamlet, a studious young man, had been at school in Germany. Though he had hurried to court as soon as he learned of his father's death, his father's brother—a schemer named Claudius—had moved even faster. Taking advantage of Hamlet's absence, he had convinced the nobles to name him king instead. Swift as he had snatched up the crown, Claudius had also snatched up Hamlet's mother, who was now his queen.

Father dead, crown lost, mother wed with unseemly haste, Hamlet found himself filled with grief and rage.

As sign of his sorrow, he dressed all in black.

When Horatio told Hamlet that a spirit in the form of his father walked the midnight ramparts, the prince was more certain than ever that something was rotten in Denmark. "I'll speak to this ghost," he vowed, "even if hell itself should gape and bid me hold my peace."

That night, as Hamlet and Horatio stood watch on the battlements, the ghost appeared once more.

"Angels and ministers of grace defend us!" cried the prince. But he gathered his courage and approached the ghost. "Be thou a spirit of health or goblin damned, you come in such a form that I must speak with thee."

The ghost beckoned to Hamlet.

The prince started to follow, but Horatio grabbed his arm. "My lord, what if it tempts you to doom?"

"Unhand me!" cried Hamlet. "I must learn what it wants of me." And shaking off Horatio, the prince followed the ghost to a private place. There it spoke to him, saying:

"I am thy father's spirit, doomed for a certain time to walk the night. In the day I am held fast in fires, until the crimes done during my life are burned away. I am forbidden to tell the secrets of death, or I could speak words that would freeze your young blood." He paused, and his face grew fierce. "O Hamlet, listen. If ever you did your father love, revenge his foul murder."

"Murder!" cried the prince in horror.

"Murder most foul," groaned the ghost. "It is given out that, sleeping in my orchard, I was serpent stung and thus died. This much is true: I was sleeping in my orchard. But the serpent who stung me was your uncle, Claudius. He poured vile poison in my ear. I died in torment, and in torment my unsanctified soul walks the earth. Your uncle has stolen my throne, my queen, my life. Avenge me, my son!"

The ghost's story fired Hamlet's heart with new rage. Yet he was also torn by doubt. The devil had many ways to trap an unwary soul. What if this spirit was not truly his father, but some clever demon sent to tempt him to murder and damnation?

Hamlet returned to Horatio and asked him to swear that he would never speak of what they had seen this night. When Horatio was too slow in his response, the voice of the ghost echoed around them, commanding, "Swear!"

"This is wondrous strange," muttered Horatio.

Hamlet put his hand on his friend's shoulder. "There are more things in heaven and earth, Horatio, than are dreamt of in your philosophy. Still, I need your silence! No matter how odd I behave in days to come, speak not of what you have seen."

For Hamlet needed to gather information before he could act on the ghost's words, and he had decided that the cloak of madness would give him cover to do so.

"Swear!" repeated the ghost.

"Rest, rest, troubled spirit," said Hamlet. "And you, dear friend, speak not of this. The time is out of joint. O cursed spite, that ever I was born to set it right."

Over the next days, great consternation grew in court as Hamlet seemed to move from mourning to melancholy to madness.

One morning the king's advisor, a windy, wordy man named Polonius, was in his private quarters, cheerfully sending a servant to spy on his son, when his daughter, Ophelia, rushed in.

"My lord, my lord," she cried, "I have been so affrighted! As I was sewing in my room Lord Hamlet stumbled in, his face pale, his eyes so wild it was as if he had just escaped from hell."

The old man knew Hamlet had been courting Ophelia—in fact, when he had learned of this, he had forbidden his daughter to see the prince, for it was his opinion that Hamlet had been merely toying with the girl. Now he wondered if he had been wrong.

"Mad for thy love?" asked Polonius.

As Ophelia described Hamlet's trembling and staring, Polonius began to suspect that the prince's vows of love had been real after all, and that Ophelia's refusal had made him insane.

The king and queen, also concerned about Hamlet, had summoned two of the prince's school friends to court.

"Good Rosencrantz, gentle Guildenstern," said Queen Gertrude when they arrived. "I beg you, visit my too much changed son and learn, if you can, the source of his sorrows."

While the royal couple waited for Rosencrantz and Guildenstern to do their spying, Polonius came to them and said, "My lord and lady, your noble son is mad. That he is mad, 'tis true; 'tis true 'tis pity, and pity 'tis 'tis true. But I will be brief, for brevity is the soul of wit. Your son loves my daughter."

"How has she received this love?" asked Claudius.

"What do you think of me, my lord?" asked Polonius, drawing himself up. "When I learned of it, I forbade it. 'Lord Hamlet is a prince out of thy star,' I told her. Then I ordered her lock herself away from him. He, thus repelled, fell into a sadness, then into a fast, thence to a weakness, and at last into the madness where now he raves."

"How may we test this further?" asked Claudius.

"He sometimes walks for hours here in the lobby," said Polonius. "I'll send my daughter to him, and we will listen from behind one of these curtains." For the old man was dearly fond of spying. "Look, here he comes now! You two away. I will test him on this matter."

When Hamlet came wandering by, book in hand, Polonius asked, "Do you know me, my lord?"

"Excellent well," said the prince. "You are a fishmonger."

"What is it that you read?" asked the old advisor, trying another tack.

"Words, words, words," replied Hamlet.

"Words about what?" asked Polonius, trying not to grow angry at the prince's nonsense.

"Why, they are slanders! This rogue claims that old men have gray beards, wrinkled faces, runny eyes, and a plentiful lack of wit!"

All of which were fair descriptions of Polonius himself.

"Though this be madness, yet there is method in it," muttered the old man. To Hamlet he said, "My lord, I will take my leave of you."

"You cannot take anything from me that I would not more willingly part with," said the prince. He paused, then added softly, "Except my life."

Next to test the prince were Rosencrantz and Guildenstern, but they had no better luck finding the true source of his strange behavior than did Polonius.

"Denmark's a prison," he told them.

"We think not so, my lord," replied Rosencrantz.

"Why then, 'tis not to you; for there is nothing either good or bad, but thinking makes it so. To me it is a prison. But enough. What brings you here to Elsinore, good friends?"

The answer—"We come to visit you, my lord; no other occasion"— came just a bit too quickly.

Catching the uneasiness in his friends' voices, Hamlet asked shrewdly, "Have the king and queen sent for you?"

The two men could not deny this.

"I will tell you why," said the prince. "I have of late lost all my mirth, so that the world appears to be nothing to me but a foul and pestilent congregation of vapors. What a piece of work is man, how infinite in faculties, in form and moving. Yet man delights me not, nor woman neither."

Appalled by this gloomy speech, Rosencrantz said, "Perhaps, my lord, you can take delight to hear that the players are coming."

This news did, indeed, cheer the melancholy prince, who was friendly with the players. When they entered the castle, he asked the lead player to recite a speech he particularly loved. This the man did, with such power and passion that tears flowed down his cheeks as he spoke his lines.

Listening, the prince hatched a new scheme. Taking the lead actor aside, he asked him to put on a play called "The Murder of Gonzago," which echoed some parts of his own father's death. He asked, too, if the actors might insert some special lines that he would write for them.

After the players had agreed and left to ready their show, Hamlet found himself in a state of despair. The passion with which the actor had delivered his speech, the tears that had sprung to the man's eyes, were like a spur to Hamlet's soul.

"What a rogue and peasant slave am I!" he cried. "Look how that man wept at a mere play. What would he do if he had the motive and cause that I have for revenge? But still, I must be certain. I have heard that a guilty man, seeing his crime, will be moved to fear, for murder has a tongue of its own, and will be heard. When they put on this show, I'll observe my false new father carefully. If the ghost's words be true, then surely Claudius will react to what he sees. The play's the thing wherein I'll catch the conscience of the king!"

Polonius, meanwhile, was pursuing his plan to have the king and queen listen in when Hamlet next saw Ophelia, for he still hoped to prove it was indeed love that had made the prince mad. With this in mind, the old man stationed his daughter in the lobby. He sent for Hamlet, then took the king and queen to hide where they could hear.

Hamlet wandered in, distracted and wondering whether he should even continue to live. "To be, or not to be," he said aloud, though speaking only to himself. "That is the question. Who would bear the whips and scorns of time when he could with bare dagger end this suffering—but that the dread of something after death, the undiscovered country, puzzles the will and forces us to bear those ills we know rather than to fly to those we know not of. Thus does conscience make cowards of us all."

Ophelia listened in sorrow. When he was done, she went to him and tried to return some small gifts he had given her.

"I never gave you anything!" he declared, pushing them away.

"My honored lord," she said gently, "you know right well you did, and with them words of so sweet breath composed as made these things more rich."

"Are you honest?" cried Hamlet. Then he began to rant at her, terrifying the girl with his seeming madness. Suddenly he asked, "Where is your father?"

"At home," she said, as she had been told to do. And with this simple lie she pierced the prince's heart, for he knew in that moment he could no longer trust her, love her though he did. Now his rage and sadness were more bitter and more real, and he soon left her.

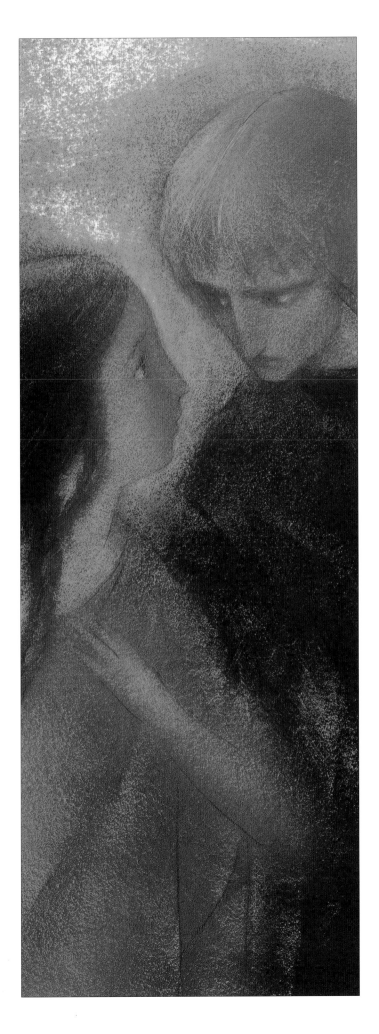

"Oh, what a noble mind is here o'erthrown," mourned Ophelia. "And I, of ladies most deject and wretched, now see that sovereign reason like sweet bells jangled, out of time and harsh."

Polonius was now convinced that the prince's strange behavior was due to neglected love. Claudius, however, remained wary. "Though what Hamlet spoke lacked form, it was not like madness. I sense something dangerous in his soul. I have resolved to send him to England, both to collect our neglected tribute, and to give his seething heart time to settle."

"It shall do," said Polonius. "Yet I still believe his grief springs from thwarted love. If you see fit, after the play have the queen speak to him alone, seeking to know his sorrows. Hidden there, I shall be your ears."

"It shall be so," said Claudius grimly. "Madness in great ones must not unwatched go."

Hamlet was busy preparing for the night's action, which he hoped would bring an end to his uncertainty.

First he advised the players on how to speak the lines he had given them. Next he drew Horatio aside and said, "Observe my uncle carefully. If in his face you see no guilt, then the ghost is false, and my imagination is to blame."

The court assembled. Hamlet, seeming in high spirits, spoke insultingly to Polonius. Then he sat next to Ophelia, but was rude to her as well.

The play began. A king and queen were discussing the king's health, the queen declaring that she could never wed another should he die.

"Methinks the lady doth protest too much," murmured Gertrude, who had wed so soon after her own husband's death.

"What do you call this play?" asked Claudius sharply.

"'The Mousetrap,'" replied Hamlet.

On stage, the player king lay down to nap. An actor entered, clutching a bottle. Tipping it at the sleeping king's ear, he murmured, "Thou mixture rank, of midnight weeds collected, do your dark and evil work."

At this, the very image of his own crime, Claudius bolted up. With a cry, he fled the room.

"Look to the king!" cried the courtiers. All rushed out to follow Claudius—all save Hamlet and Horatio.

"Did you see?" crowed Hamlet. "Now I'll take the ghost's word for good."

"My lord," said Rosencrantz, returning with Guildenstern at his side. "Your mother is most vexed with you. Your behavior has struck her into amazement."

"She bids you come to her chambers," added Guildenstern.

"I'll to her by and by. Now leave me!" ordered Hamlet, with new fire and force. When he was alone, he turned his head to the skies, clenched his fists, and said, "'Tis now the very witching time of night, when churchyards yawn and hell itself breathes out contagion. Now could I drink hot blood and do such bitter business as the day would quake to look on. To my mother, then. I will speak daggers to her."

As he walked the halls, he passed an open door. Through it he spied Claudius, whose guilty conscience had driven him to fall to his knees and pray. Now might I kill him, thought Hamlet with grim satisfaction. For his guilt is sure and I have the opportunity.

Yet there was a new problem: If Claudius were killed while praying, his soul would go straight to heaven, which was the last thing Hamlet wanted. Regretfully, he left the praying king and hurried to his mother's chambers, where she awaited him with Polonius hiding behind the curtain.

"Now, Mother," said Hamlet when he came in. "What's the matter?"

"Hamlet, you have your father much offended."

"Mother, you have my father much offended."

"You answer with an idle tongue!" said the queen.

"You question with a wicked tongue," replied Hamlet angrily. "Now sit you down, for you shall not budge until I set up a mirror to show your inmost heart." He began to berate her, growing so enraged that the queen cried out in fear.

Hearing her fright, Polonius called, "What, ho! Help!"

"A rat!" shouted Hamlet. Thinking it was Claudius hiding behind the curtain, he drew his sword and thrust it through. What horror the prince felt when out fell the body of Polonius, and he saw that he had killed the father of the girl he loved.

"What a rash and bloody deed is this!" sobbed the queen.

Hamlet turned on her with new fury. "A bloody deed? Almost as bad, good mother, as kill a king and marry his brother."

But as Hamlet ranted, he felt a cold chill. Looking up, he saw the ghost of his father. "Do you come your tardy son to chide?" asked the prince fearfully.

"Alas, he's mad," whispered the queen, who saw not the ghost.

"Your quarrel is not with your mother," intoned the spirit. "It is Claudius you must deal with! Do not forget!"

Yet revenge would now be harder, for when Claudius learned of Polonius's death, he had the perfect excuse to send Hamlet to England. "For your own safety you need be gone until we can deal with the uproar that will follow this slaying," he said, feigning sorrow at Hamlet's exile. But Claudius had deeper plans than merely getting Hamlet out of Denmark. Summoning Rosencrantz and Guildenstern, he privately asked them to accompany the prince, and to carry a sealed letter to the English king, who was under Denmark's control.

Unknown to the two men, the letter ordered the immediate death of Prince Hamlet.

Ophelia, having lost her father to an act of violence by the man she loved, fell into a madness true, not feigned. She began to wander the halls of Elsinore, flowers in hand, singing strange and mournful songs.

Gertrude and Claudius, already uneasy, felt their world cracking around them when Ophelia's brother, Laertes—who had been away in Paris—returned at the head of a mob.

"I demand justice for my father's death!" he cried.

But Claudius knew how to play on men's hearts, and with honeyed words he calmed the angry youth, convincing him that his true enemy was Prince Hamlet.

As they spoke, Ophelia wandered in, her eyes vacant, her mind gone. The sight of his poor sister nearly broke Laertes's heart. "O heat, dry up my brains!" he moaned. "Is it possible a young maid's wits should be as mortal as an old man's life?"

All Ophelia did was sing, her voice high, sweet, and mad.

Thus did Laertes's hatred for Hamlet rise to fever pitch.

As for the prince, his trip to England was interrupted when pirates attacked their ship. Fighting ferociously—for here was a clear and present foe, with no impediment to action—Hamlet leaped aboard the pirate vessel, the first from his ship to do so. When the two ships separated, he was held prisoner. But in return for a favor he did them, the pirates set the prince back on Denmark's coast. Quickly he sent a letter to Horatio, who hurried to his side.

When Claudius received word that Hamlet was back, he decided to do what the prince had so far been unable to do: Take swift action to kill his enemy. Drawing Laertes aside, he said, "What would you do to Hamlet to show yourself your father's son?"

"Cut his throat in church!" growled Laertes.

Claudius knew he had his man. "Here is what we will do instead. I will arrange, by reports of your excellence, to have the two of you brought together for a fencing match. Sport only, it shall seem. But among the blades that will be offered you, I will have hidden one that is not blunted. Choose you that. Then, when you kill him during the fight, it will look like no more than a sad accident!"

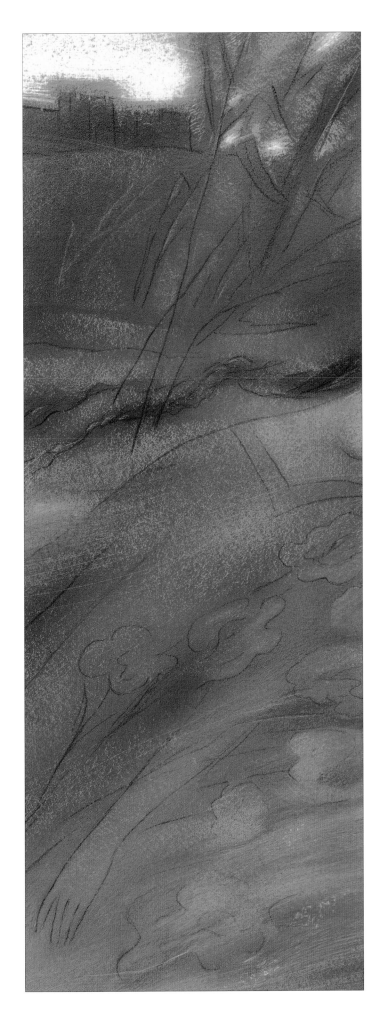

Laertes gladly agreed, adding, "To make sure he dies, I'll smear the blade with poison." Claudius, eager to leave nothing to chance, decided to also prepare a poisoned drink that he would offer Hamlet during the duel.

Their scheming was interrupted by a wail of despair from Queen Gertrude, who rushed in, crying, "Your sister's drowned, Laertes."

"Drowned?" he echoed in horror. "Oh, where?"

"There is a willow beside the brook where Ophelia tried to hang a garland of flowers. A branch broke beneath her and she plunged into the water. Too wrapped in madness to save herself, she floated along, clutching her flowers and singing, until her clothes weighed her down, and pulled her from song to muddy death."

With this report, the rage that Laertes felt toward his former friend Hamlet grew more murderous than ever.

The next day Horatio and Hamlet, unaware of Ophelia's death, were making their way to Elsinore. Crossing the graveyard near the castle, they came upon a gravedigger, singing at his work. As he dug, he flung up bones from previous burials. The sight turned Hamlet's thoughts once more toward death. Picking up a skull, he asked the gravedigger if he knew whom it belonged to.

"Aye, it was that mad jester, Yorick."

Hamlet sighed. "Alas, poor Yorick! I knew him, Horatio. A fellow of infinite jest. He used to take me on his back when I was a child, and set the table on a roar with his foolery."

The prince's musings were interrupted by the approach of a funeral procession. "Come," murmured Hamlet, and the two young men slipped into the nearby trees, to avoid being seen. They were startled to see that it was a royal funeral, led by the king and queen—and even more startled that it was brief, and with little ceremony.

Their surprise at this brevity was echoed by Laertes, who stood at the head of the grave. "Is there to be no more?" he demanded.

"We have done as much as church allows," replied the priest. "It would profane the service of the dead to do more for one who may have been self-slaughtered."

Laertes was furious. "I tell thee, churlish priest, a ministering angel shall my sister be when thou liest howling!"

And this was how Hamlet learned that they were burying his beloved Ophelia.

The queen stepped to the edge of the grave. "Sweets to the sweet," she said, scattering flowers over the body.

The gravedigger lifted his shovel.

But Laertes leaped into the grave, crying, "Hold off the earth awhile, till I have caught her once more in mine arms!" Then he lifted the body of his dead sister for one last embrace.

Hamlet could contain himself no longer. Bursting from the woods, he leaped into the grave himself, shouting, "Forty thousand brothers could not love Ophelia as I did!"

Now Laertes saw not his one-time friend, but the man who had killed his father and driven his sister to madness. He lunged at Hamlet, tightening his hands about the prince's neck.

"Pull them apart!" ordered the king as the queen cried out in fear.

When the guards had separated the two men, Claudius asked Horatio to watch over the prince. Then he led the royal party back to the castle.

Hamlet and Horatio also continued to Elsinore. As they walked, Hamlet gave his friend further evidence of the king's treachery: "When I was on the ship, I went one night to the cabin where Rosencrantz and Guildenstern were sleeping. From their bags I retrieved the letter my uncle had given them. It ordered the English king to have me killed! After some thought, I replaced it with another letter, ordering the deaths of Rosencrantz and Guildenstern."

Hamlet and Horatio were still discussing this at the castle when a foppish messenger named Osric brought a request from Claudius, summoning Hamlet to duel with Laertes.

"The king has placed a wager that you will prevail in such a contest," said the messenger—words chosen by Claudius to spur Hamlet into accepting the challenge.

The court gathered for the duel. Before it began, Hamlet made gracious apologies to Laertes for the grief he had unintentionally brought to his family, and they stated a renewed friendship. Even so, when the swords were offered to Laertes, he chose the poison-smeared blade.

At the same time Claudius prepared the poisoned chalice.

The duel began. After a few passes, Claudius offered Hamlet a drink. When he refused, the queen took the cup and cried, "I drink to you, Hamlet!"

As she raised the cup to her lips, Claudius made as if to stop her. But he could not reveal that the cup held poison without confessing his own guilt. Frozen with horror, he watched in cowardly silence as she drank the lethal potion.

The fight resumed. The men were young and strong, and their blades wove a silver net in the air. Suddenly Laertes scored a point, cutting Hamlet with the poisoned blade.

Hamlet, stung by his wound and enraged by the realization that Laertes was using an unprotected sword, fought more fiercely than ever. They engaged in a close fight and as they scuffled, the blades were switched. A moment later Hamlet scored a hit on Laertes, wounding him with the poisoned blade that Laertes himself had coated.

Now Laertes knew that both he and Hamlet were doomed. But before he could speak, someone shouted, "The queen! Look to the queen!"

All turned toward Gertrude. Her eyes were wide, her skin pale. "O my dear Hamlet! It was the drink. I am poisoned!" With these words she collapsed and died.

"More treachery!" cried Hamlet. "Let the door be locked."

"The king's to blame!" gasped Laertes, who was staggering now himself. "The king has poisoned the queen, and you are poisoned too, Hamlet, for that blade with which I wounded you was smeared with venom. In thee there is not half an hour's life."

Now, at last, Hamlet was moved to action. Roaring with fury he ran the king through with the poisoned blade. Snatching up the cup, he forced it to the king's lips, crying, "Here, thou damned, murderous Dane, drink off this potion! Follow my mother!"

Double-poisoned, Claudius shuddered and fell dead.

Laertes held out a trembling hand. "Exchange forgiveness with me, noble Hamlet. Mine and my father's death come not upon thee in judgment. Let not your death come upon me."

"Heaven make thee free of it!" said Hamlet gently. Turning, he cried, "I am dead, Horatio. Wretched queen, adieu! This fell sergeant, Death, is strict in his arrest. Oh, I could tell you—but let it be. Horatio, I am dead. You, who live, report my cause."

But Horatio wished to follow his friend to that unknown country. "There's yet some liquor left," he said, lifting the poisoned chalice.

Hamlet caught his hand. "If ever thou didst hold me in thy heart, then stay in this harsh world to tell my story."

As he spoke, they heard the sound of distant drums. Fortinbras and his Norwegian army were marching on Elsinore.

"I die, Horatio," said Hamlet softly. "Fortinbras shall be king." He tightened his grip on Horatio's hand. "Tell my story," he whispered again.

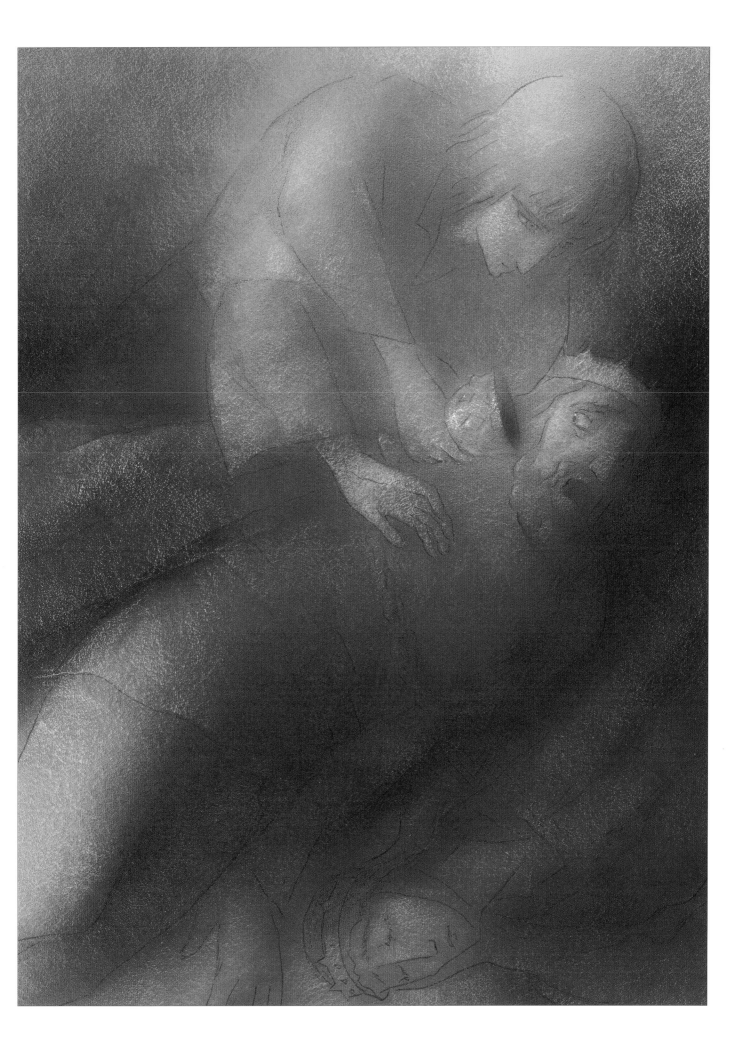

Then life fled him.

Weeping, Horatio knelt beside Hamlet's body. "Now cracks a noble heart," whispered the true friend. "Good night, sweet prince, and flights of angels sing thee to thy rest."

When Fortinbras and his men marched into the court, they were astonished at the bloody scene that met their eyes. "O proud death," said the warrior, "how have you so many princes at one shot so bloodily struck?"

"That can I reveal," said Horatio. "And much more. Let these bodies be placed high on a stage, and I will tell the yet unknowing world the tale of Hamlet, Prince of Denmark, and the tragedy that befell him."

———————

And so in this one thing alone did Hamlet find his way,
for his story was told, and retold, and told again,
as it is unto this very day.